To:

From:

Little Bird Finds CHRISTMAS

Written by

Marianne Richmond

Illustrations by Janet Samuel

Text © 2022 by Marianne Richmond
Illustrations by Janet Samuel
Cover and internal design and illustrations © 2022 by Sourcebooks

Sourcebooks and the colophon are registered trademarks of Sourcebooks.

Adobe Photoshop was used to prepare the full color art.

Published by Sourcebooks Jabberwocky, an imprint of Sourcebooks Kids
P.O. Box 4410, Naperville, Illinois 60567–4410
(630) 961-3900
sourcebookskids.com

Cataloging-in-Publication Data is on file with the Library of Congress.

Source of Production: Worzalla, Stevens Point, Wisconsin, USA
Date of Production: July 2022
Run Number: 5024693

Printed and bound in United States of America
WOZ 10 9 8 7 6 5 4 3 2 1

Dedicated to my family, who makes it easy
to find Christmas wherever we are.
—MR

For my family.
—JS

Mama and Little Bird cuddled in their nest,
warm and cozy against the December chill.

"Christmas is coming soon," Mama whispered.
Little Bird sat up wide awake. "Then let's go find it!" she said.
"Except it's time for bed," Mama laughed and closed her eyes.

When Little Bird woke up, Mama was gone.

Little Bird ate her breakfast
and fluffed her bed.

Then she waited. (And not
very patiently.) She could
not stop thinking about
Christmas coming, though
she didn't know exactly
what it looked like.

"I will find Christmas myself!" she said, and she flew away.

First, Little Bird went to the Big Store.
Sparkly trees tickled the ceiling, happy music filled the air, and excited
children waited to meet a jolly man in a red-and-white suit.

SANTA'S VILLAGE

TOY SHOP

Little Bird peeked into store after store looking for Christmas.

Instead, she saw people carrying large bags filled with toys and goodies.

"Christmas isn't here," she decided, and she flew away.

Next, Little Bird went to the Food Market. The parking lot overflowed with cars. Yummy smells greeted her nose, and moms and dads pushed carts piled high with delicious food.

Little Bird looked for Christmas in every aisle, on every shelf, and in every cart and grocery bag.

"I have SO much to do for Christmas!" the delighted people said to one another. "Wherever it is," sighed Little Bird, and she flew away from here, too.

Finally, Little Bird went to the Post Office.
A long line of people curved around the corner,
holding stacks of letters and packages.

"Are they waiting to see Christmas?" Little Bird wondered.
She peered inside, and she saw three busy helpers behind
the counter.
And none of them looked like Christmas.

Little Bird sat on a branch to rest.
"Where are you, Christmas?" she said aloud.

"I'll show you," said a familiar voice in the tree.

"Mama?" said Little Bird, surprised.

"Yes," she said. "I've been following close behind you."

"I'm trying to find Christmas," Little Bird explained.

"It's not at the Big Store.

It's not at the Food Market.

And it's not at the Post Office."

"Oh, but it is!" said Mama. "Let me show you!"
And they flew away together.

Mama stopped at the Beautiful Church in the Village.
"Christmas," she said, "is the day we celebrate the birth of Jesus, who is the son of God. God sent Jesus to earth as His gift of love to the world."

"Is Jesus in there now?" asked Little Bird.
"Oh no!" laughed Mama. "Jesus lived a long time ago,
but God's love is still with us every day."

"Okay," said Little Bird. "But where do we *find* Christmas?"
She had looked in a lot of places, and she was tired.

"In your own heart," said Mama. "In my heart. In all the grateful, giving hearts. It's our thank-you back to God for His gift of love to us."

"If Christmas is in our hearts," Little Bird asked, "why are so many people at the Big Store, the Food Market, and the Post Office?"

"Because," said Mama, "when you have a thankful heart, you want to share the love of Christmas by giving gifts, gathering together, and remembering faraway family and friends."

Little Bird was beginning to understand that Christmas wasn't so hard to find after all!

Back in their warm and cozy nest, Mama and Little Bird cuddled against the December chill.

"Want to know *my* favorite place to find Christmas?" asked Mama.
"I do," said Little Bird.
"With you," Mama said.

In the morning, Mama nudged Little Bird awake.
"Christmas is here!" said Mama.
But Little Bird already knew this.
She didn't need to go looking anymore.

She found Christmas.
In her heart.
Right where she was.

Photo © Shoott Photography

MARIANNE RICHMOND is a bestselling author and artist who has touched the lives of millions for more than two decades by creating books that celebrate the love of family. Visit her at mariannerichmond.com.

"My books help you share your heart and connect with those you love."

XO, M.

JANET SAMUEL is an illustrator living in a small town in South Wales, UK, with her daughter, Alice, and her scruffy terrier, Tilly. In the sixteen years she has been illustrating, she has been fortunate to illustrate books for Macmillan, Usborne, Little Tiger Press, Scholastic, and Lion Hudson amongst a few. She is at her happiest with a pencil or computer mouse in hand.